Words to Know Before You Read

chattering

complaining

ficus

hatchlings

hide-a-way

snatch

sneak

stow

suspect

vanishing

www.rourkeeducationalmedia.com

Edited by Precious McKenzie
Illustrated by Anita DuFalla
Art Direction and Page Layout by Renee Brady

Library of Congress PCN Data

Monkey Business / J. Jean Robertson
ISBN 978-1-61810-189-1 (hard cover) (alk. paper)
ISBN 978-1-61810-322-2 (soft cover)
Library of Congress Control Number: 2012936789

Rourke Educational Media
Printed in China, Artwood Press Limited,
  Shenzhen, China

rourkeeducationalmedia.com

customerservice@rourkeeducationalmedia.com   •   PO Box 643328 Vero Beach, Florida 32964

MONKEY BUSINESS

By J. Jean Robertson

Illustrated by Anita DuFalla

4

Mike and Spike are twins. Their mother, Merrilyn Monkey, is very proud of them. Their neighbor, Gabby Gator, is surprised that Merrilyn has only two babies. Gabby's nest has more little hatchlings than she can count.

Mike and Spike play games with each other and with their jungle friends. One day, while chasing their friends, Cooper Cub and Connie Cub, they find a wonderful hide-a-way. It is a cave. The opening is hidden by a big ficus plant.

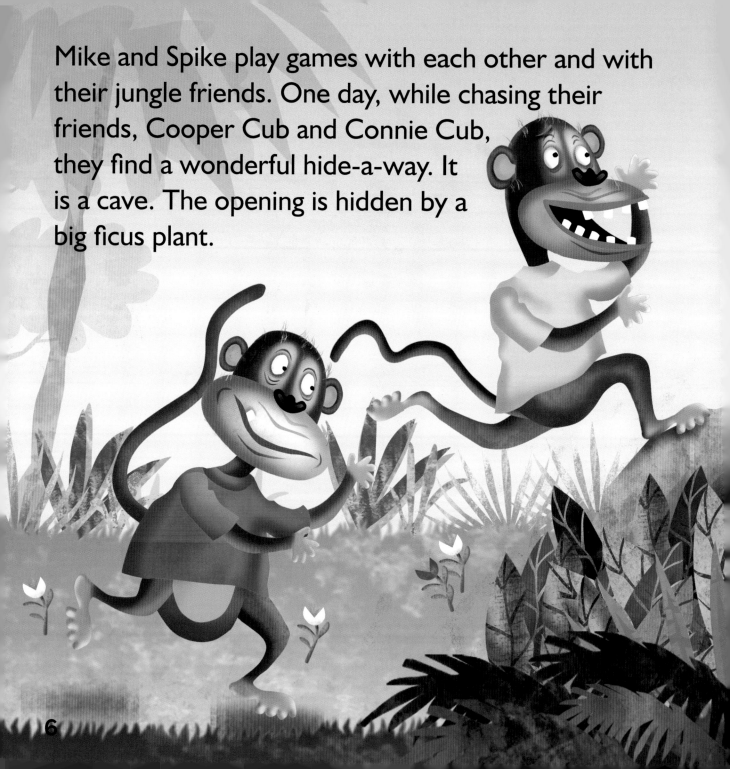

The cave gives Mike and Spike an idea for a new game. They call the game Snatch and Stow.

The object of the game is to sneak something that belongs to someone else and hide it in a secret hide-a-way.

Merrilyn begins to notice things missing from her store of special treats. She asks around the neighborhood, but finds no clues. She does not suspect her cute twin sons.

"What is all that chattering in the forest?" asks Gerry Giraffe. "It is Shirley Squirrel complaining because nuts have been disappearing from her storage bin," answers Gabby Gator.

Tyler Tiger lets out a big howl when he cannot find his new striped coat.

14

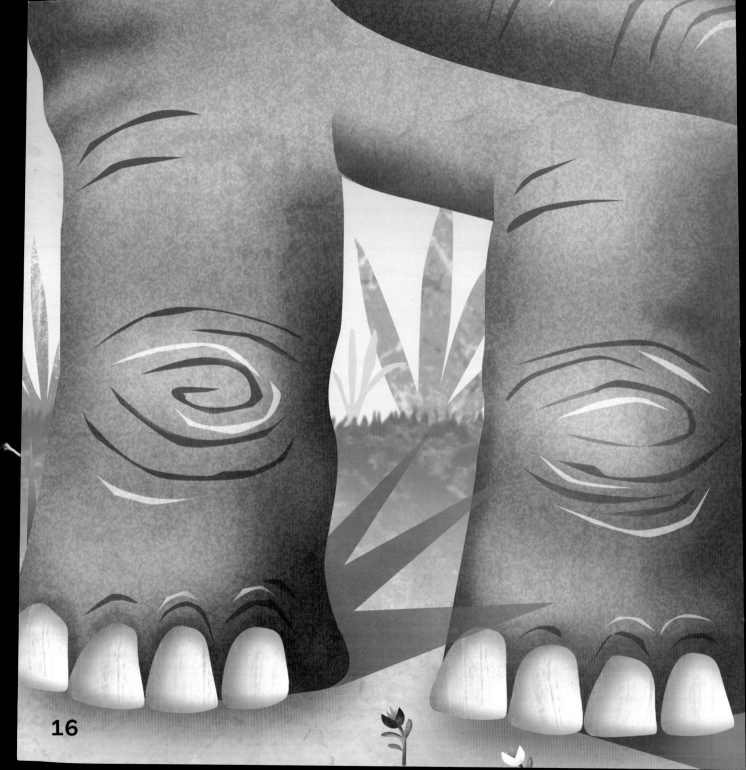

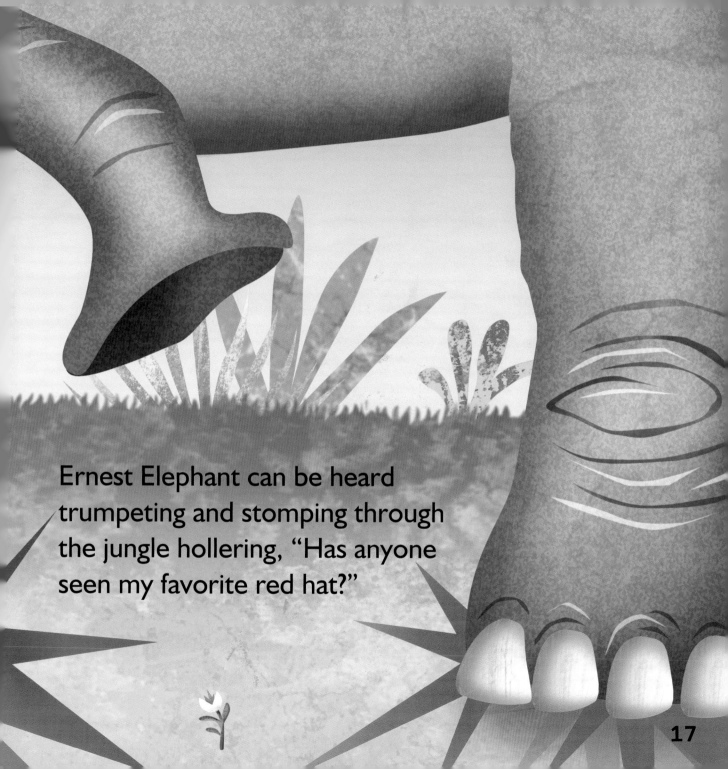

Ernest Elephant can be heard trumpeting and stomping through the jungle hollering, "Has anyone seen my favorite red hat?"

18

The jungle animals decide to call a meeting to discuss the problem of the vanishing items. "It is dishonest to take people's things," says Homer Warthog. "Let's ask Merrilyn to make a list of who has lost what."

WHO

Merrilyn Monkey
Shirley Squirrel
Tyler Tiger
Ernest Elephant
Gabby Gator
Homer Warthog
Gerry Giraffe

WHAT

Special Treats
Nuts
New Striped Coat
Favorite Red Hat
Giant Tooth Brush
Sunglasses
Green Tie

When Ernest suggests that they divide into teams to hunt for their missing items, Mike whispers, "Mama, we don't need to go looking. Spike and I know where everything is. It was part of our Snatch and Stow game."

Spike hollers, "Come on everybody, we'll show you! Everything's in our hide-a-way cave. It's all safe, and sound, and found." The twins promise not to play Snatch and Stow ever again.

After Reading Activities

You and the Story...

Why were the jungle animals missing things?

Why do you think Mike and Spike promised not to play Snatch and Stow ever again?

Do you think Mike and Spike were sorry they snitched people's things?

Would you be sorry if you learned that something you had done was dishonest?

Words You Know Now...

Three of the words you now know are scrambled below. Find them and write them on a piece of paper.

tows	singhhlact	sucif
chattering	hide-a-way	suspect
complaining	snatch	vanishing
ficus	sneak	
hatchlings	stow	

You Could...Make Up a New Game to Play

- Ask your friends to help you think of ideas for a new game.

- Make a list of the ideas.

- Vote to choose which game to play.

- Make a list of things you might need for your game.

- Choose a name for your game.

- Play your new game with your friends.

About the Author

J. Jean Robertson, also known as Bushka to her grandchildren and many other kids, lives in San Antonio, Florida with her husband. She is retired after many years of teaching. She loves to read, travel, and write books for children.

Ask The Author!
www.rem4students.com

About the Illustrator

Acclaimed for its versatility in style, Anita DuFalla's work has appeared in many educational books, newspaper articles, and business advertisements and on numerous posters, book and magazine covers, and even giftwraps. Anita's passion for pattern is evident in both her artwork and her collection of 400 patterned tights. She lives in the Friendship neighborhood of Pittsburgh, Pennsylvania with her son, Lucas.